Guelph Public Library

J915.957 DAN
Daniels-Cowart, Catrina, author.
Singapore

Guelph Public Library

ASIAN COUNTRIES TODAY

SINGAPORE

ASIAN COUNTRIES TODAY

CHINA
INDONESIA
JAPAN
MALAYSIA
PHILIPPINES
SINGAPORE
SOUTH KOREA
THAILAND
VIETNAM

ASIAN COUNTRIES TODAY

SINGAPORE

CATRINA
DANIELS-COWART

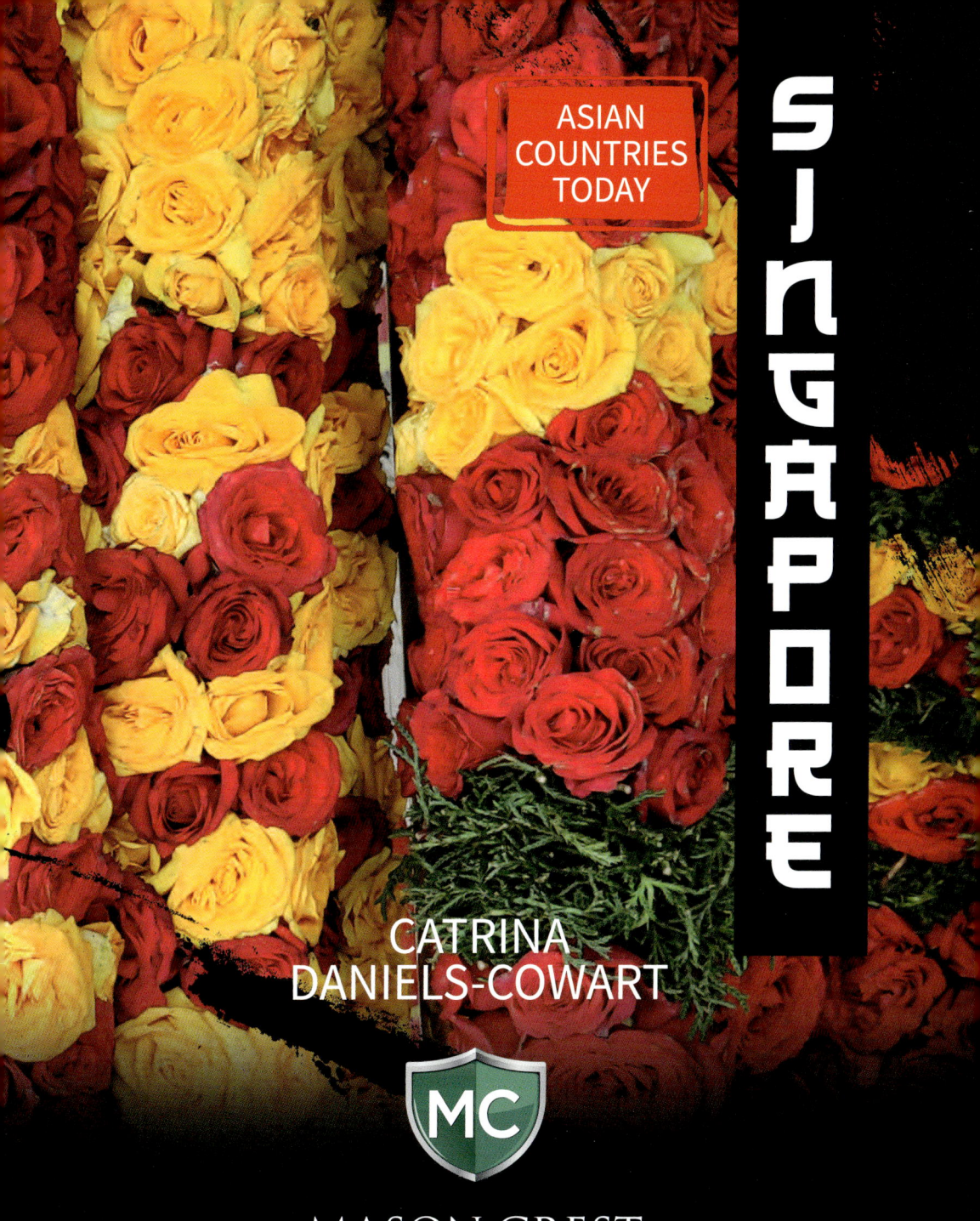

MASON CREST
PHILADELPHIA
MIAMI

MASON CREST

450 Parkway Drive, Suite D, Broomall, Pennsylvania 19008
(866) MCP-BOOK (toll-free) • www.masoncrest.com

Copyright © 2020 by Mason Crest, an imprint of National Highlights, Inc. All rights reserved. No part of this publication may be reproduced or transmitted in any form or by any means, electronic or mechanical, including photocopying, recording, taping or any information storage and retrieval system, without permission in writing from the publisher.

Printed in the United States of America

First printing
9 8 7 6 5 4 3 2 1

ISBN (hardback) 978-1-4222-4270-4
ISBN (series) 978-1-4222-4263-6
ISBN (ebook) 978-1-4222-7556-6

Cataloging-in-Publication Data on file with the Library of Congress

Developed and Produced by National Highlights Inc.
Editor: Susan Uttendorfsky
Interior and cover design: Jana Rade
Production: Michelle Luke

NATIONAL HIGHLIGHTS

QR CODES AND LINKS TO THIRD-PARTY CONTENT

You may gain access to certain third-party content ("Third-Party Sites") by scanning and using the QR Codes that appear in this publication (the "QR Codes"). We do not operate or control in any respect any information, products, or services on such Third-Party Sites linked to by us via the QR Codes included in this publication, and we assume no responsibility for any materials you may access using the QR Codes. Your use of the QR Codes may be subject to terms, limitations, or restrictions set forth in the applicable terms of use or otherwise established by the owners of the Third-Party Sites. Our linking to such Third-Party Sites via the QR Codes does not imply an endorsement or sponsorship of such Third-Party Sites or the information, products, or services offered on or through the Third-Party Sites, nor does it imply an endorsement or sponsorship of this publication by the owners of such Third-Party Sites.

CONTENTS

Singapore at a Glance.. 6
Chapter 1: Singapore's Geography & Landscape...................... 11
Chapter 2: The Government & History of Singapore 19
Chapter 3: Singapore's Economy 29
Chapter 4: Citizens of Singapore—
People, Customs & Culture 45
Chapter 5: Famous Cities of Singapore...................................... 67
Chapter 6: A Bright Future for Singapore 77
Singaporean Food... 82
Festivals & Holidays... 86
Series Glossary of Key Terms.. 88
Chronology... 90
Further Reading & Internet Resources... 91
Index... 92
Organizations to Contact... 95
Author's Biography & Credits.. 96

KEY ICONS TO LOOK FOR:

WORDS TO UNDERSTAND: These words with their easy-to-understand definitions will increase the reader's understanding of the text while building vocabulary skills.

SIDEBARS: This boxed material within the main text allows readers to build knowledge, gain insights, explore possibilities, and broaden their perspectives by weaving together additional information to provide realistic and holistic perspectives.

EDUCATIONAL VIDEOS: Readers can view videos by scanning our QR codes, providing them with additional educational content to supplement the text. Examples include news coverage, moments in history, speeches, iconic sports moments, and much more!

TEXT-DEPENDENT QUESTIONS: These questions send the reader back to the text for more careful attention to the evidence presented there.

RESEARCH PROJECTS: Readers are pointed toward areas of further inquiry connected to each chapter. Suggestions are provided for projects that encourage deeper research and analysis.

SERIES GLOSSARY OF KEY TERMS: This back-of-the-book glossary contains terminology used throughout this series. Words found here increase the reader's ability to read and comprehend higher-level books and articles in this field.

SINGAPORE AT A GLANCE

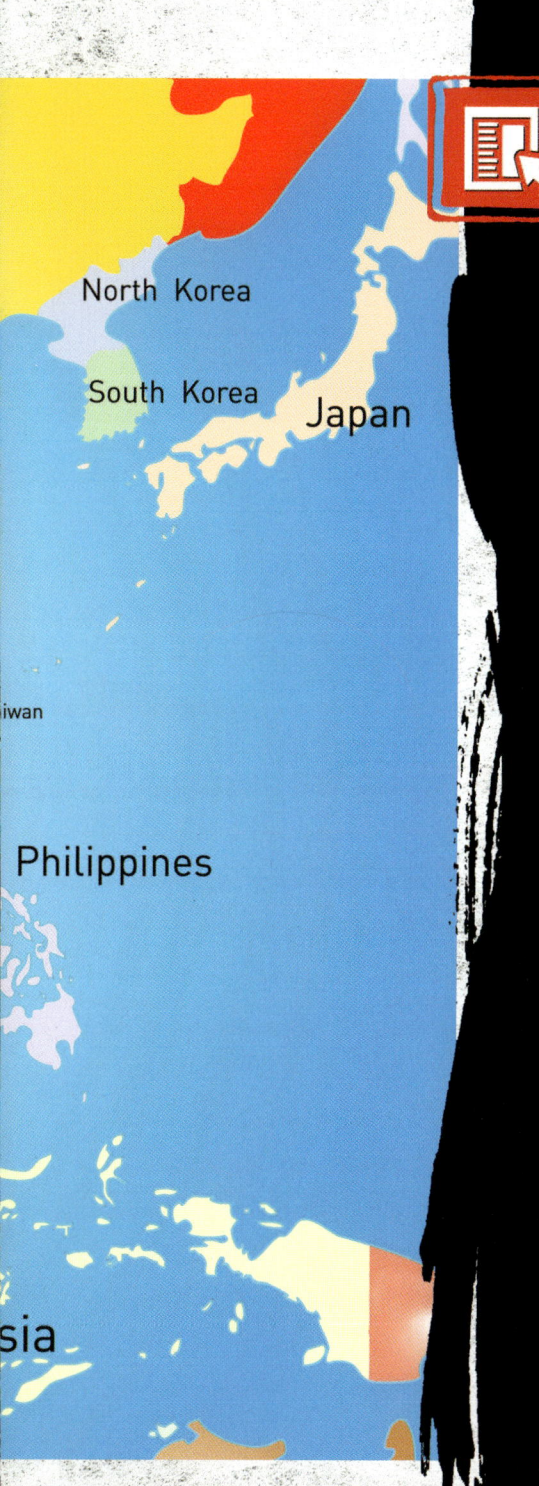

The Geography of Singapore

Location: Southeastern Asia, located between Malaysia and Indonesia

Area: Around 3.5 times the size of Washington, D.C.
total: 277.68 square miles (719.2 sq. km)
land: 273.82 square miles (709.2 sq. km))
water: 3.9 square miles (10 sq. km)

Borders: None

Climate: Tropical—rainy, humid, and hot. There are two monsoon seasons, the northeastern monsoon from December through March, and the southwestern from June through September. The seasons between monsoons frequently generate afternoon and early evening thunderstorms

Terrain: A gradually undulating central plateau with low-lying features

Elevation Extremes:
lowest point: Singapore Strait, 0 feet (0 m), exactly at sea level
highest point: Bukit Timah, 544 feet (166 m) above sea level

Natural Hazards:
Flash flooding

Source: www.cia.gov 2017

FLAG OF SINGAPORE

Singapore's flag is fairly simple, consisting of two horizontal stripes that split the flag in half. Red is on the top, with white on the bottom. The red represents the equality of men, as well as brotherhood. White stands for purity and virtue. The upper left corner has a white image of a crescent moon and five stars forming a circle within its points.

The flag was adopted in 1959, the year that the country became self-governing while still part of the British Empire. When the nation became independent in 1965, the flag was reconfirmed. Prior to 2004, individuals and nongovernmental organizations were not allowed to fly the flag except during the month of August, which marks the country's anniversary of independence. That rule has since been relaxed.

The People of Singapore

Population: 5,995,991

Ethnic Groups: Chinese, Indian, Malay, other

Age Structure:
0–14 years: 12.77% (765,480)
15–24 years: 16.05% (962,565)
25–54 years: 50.61% (39,300,133)
55–64 years: 6.04% (3,034,7075)
65 years and over: 10.53% (590,590)

Population Growth Rate: 1.79%

Death Rate: 3.5 deaths/1,000 pop.

Migration Rate: 13.1 migrant(s)/1,000 pop.

Infant Mortality Rate: 2.3 deaths/1,000 live births

Life Expectancy at Birth:
total population: 85.5 years
male: 82.8 years
female: 88.3 years

Total Fertility Rate: 0.84 children born/woman

Religions: Buddhist, 33.2%, Muslim, 14%, Taoist, 10%, Hindu, 5%, Christian, 18.8%, other, .06%, none, 18.5%

Languages: English, Mandarin, Malay, Chinese dialects, Tamil

Literacy Rate: 97%

Source: www.cia.gov 2017

Saint John's Island is south of the mainland of Singapore. It is a popular destination for tourists.

WORDS TO UNDERSTAND

estuarine: relating to, or formed at, that part of a river in which the current meets the sea's tide

intermonsoonal: between two monsoon seasons

squalls: brief but sudden violent windstorms that are usually accompanied by snow, sleet, or rain

surges: strong, forward movements

10 SINGAPORE

SINGAPORE'S GEOGRAPHY & LANDSCAPE

CHAPTER 1

Singapore has beautiful geography that entices people around the globe. Perhaps due to its location and ideal weather conditions, it has become a hot spot for tourists and businesses alike. It has unique flora and fauna, and it has predictable seasons. Although the country is small, it makes the most of its space and is easy to travel through.

Geography

Around two-thirds of the main island of Singapore is less than 50 feet (15.25 meters) above sea level, which makes it prone to flash flooding from heavy rainstorms. The highest summit on the island is Timah Hill, which only extends 531 feet (161.82 meters) upward. While the terrain is sometimes rugged in the center of the island, the eastern section of the island is a low plateau with hills and valleys.

Flooding can be severe in Singapore due to streams with low gradients and because of the runoff that travels from cleared lands. Mangroves and estuaries are common, particularly surrounding the streams that head northward. There has been significant degradation of the soils in eastern Singapore due to their infertile nature. Erosion has depleted them.

The Climate

Singapore is located near the equator, which means it's in the perfect place for a tropical climate. It receives abundant rainfall and has uniform temperatures, so residents know what to expect year-round. High humidity exists throughout the year—around 80 percent—but it can vary from hour to hour.

The monsoon seasons in Singapore are separated by **intermonsoonal** periods that occur between late March and the beginning of June, and again between the end of September and early December.

A few things can affect the weather in Singapore:

- Monsoon **surges**
- Afternoon and evening thunderstorms
- **Squalls** coming from the direction of Sumatra, aka "Sumatra Squalls"

Each year, the first monsoon season falls between December and early March and

Rainfall in Singapore

Rain is a common part of life in Singapore, even if it's only for a few hours a day. It rains an average of 167 out of 365 days every year. The rain is normally heavy and accompanied by thunder. Interestingly, the number of days with rain is fairly standard all year, with somewhere between 8 and 19 days per month having rainstorms or showers. Rainfall is markedly less between February and October compared to the wetter months of November, December, and January.

Part of the reason that Singapore has so many showers is that it is extremely humid. Relative humidity in Singapore hovers around an average of 80 percent, but it has been known to reach almost 100 percent.

is called the Northeast Monsoon Season. The prevailing winds are northerly to northeasterly. It is normal to see heavy rainfall throughout the nation thanks to monsoon surges.

The first intermonsoonal season, from late March through May, sometimes has thunderstorms, and afternoon temperatures can rise above 90 degrees F (32 degrees C). For the most part, the winds in this period are light and variable.

Following this is the Southwest Monsoon Season, which is marked by southeasterly to southerly winds and Sumatra squalls with wind gusts between 25–50 mph (40–80 kph). There are sometimes showers and thunderstorms during the afternoons.

Finally there is the intermonsoonal season from October through November. Similar to the other intermonsoonal period, thunderstorms are possible. It is a bit wetter during the second intermonsoonal period than during the first.

Heavy rainfall is common in Singapore, particularly during the monsoon season.

Fauna and Flora

Before New Singapore was founded in 1819, the entire country was covered by lowland tropical forests, and mangroves and swamp forests with freshwater were common. Today, urbanization has changed the appearance of Singapore. Many of the plants that were once endemic are no longer present. Large mammals, as well as animals in tidal and **estuarine** habitats, have also been decreasing in number as land is being reclaimed from rivers and the sea. Even mangroves have become few and far between due to human influences, and now are most commonly found only in Pulau Semakau, Pulau Ubin, and Pulau Tekong. To find tropical lowlands and an evergreen rainforest, people have to visit Bukit Timah Nature Reserve.

Fortunately, despite the fact that there has been significant urbanization, Singapore still has much biodiversity. There are around 3,000 hectares of nature

A short song about Singapore and the locations of its cities.

Bukit Timah Nature Reserve is in the center of Singapore. It is located on the slopes of Bukit Timah Hill—the highest point in Singapore.

reserves throughout the country, some of which include Central Catchment Nature Reserve, Sungei Buloh Wetland Reserve, and Labrador Nature Reserve.

There are some dominant tree families to be found in Bukit Timah, particularly those of the *Dipterocarpaceae* plant family, which are tropical hardwoods. These amazing trees can grow up to 131 feet (40 meters) tall.

Two main areas of mangrove forest include Pasir Risk Park and Sungei Buhol Nature Park. The *Berembang*, a species of tree, is only able to be found in Sungei Seletar and woodlands. Mangrove cedar, mangrove fern, and pneumatophores (root systems) are all common in these areas.

Rare mangrove plant species also exist in Singapore. These include the black mangrove, milky mangrove, mangrove palm, and looking-glass mangrove.

There are approximately eighty types of mammals in Singapore, with another 110 species of reptiles and 300 species of birds. Around 600 species of freshwater fish live there as well. Most animals can only be found on nature reserves and forested areas in Pulau Teking and Pulau Ubin.

SINGAPORE'S GEOGRAPHY & LANDSCAPE

Other interesting species that can be found in Singapore include the Common Posy, a type of butterfly. The inch-long (2.5 centimeters-long) giant forest ant is one of over 73,000 kinds of insects in the country. Termites are also common and active all year. Reptiles include geckos, the reticulated python, and the paradise tree snake. Some particular birds are the olive-winged bulbul, the racket-tailed drongo, and the fairy-bluebird. Mammal species include the Malayan anteater, the Malayan flying lemur, and the common tree shrew.

Fish are abundant in Singapore, although some are unusual. Air-breathing snakeheads stay in smaller streams and low-level oxygen areas, while forest bettas—who hatch their eggs inside their mouths—travel along streams and other waterways. The harlequin rasbora is a famous fish from Singapore that manages to survive in local streams and waterways.

Harlequin Rasbora
(pictured right)

The harlequin rasbora is a simple little fish with beautiful coloration in its metallic appearance. It's orange and black in many cases, and it can often be kept in community tanks if people wish to have them in their own homes. This fish is native to Singapore, and it is known to inhabit water in areas where there is a high concentration of humic matter (essentially in peat swamp forests). The fish also survives well where there is low mineral content.

There are five dozen types of rasbora, but the harlequin is the most popular. It is reddish-copper, appearing orange in many cases, and has a black wedge coloring its rear half. These fish usually travel in schools of eight to ten or more and are peaceful with one another. What makes this fish more interesting is that it's extremely hard to breed. They like to eat live foods, like mosquito larvae, before they spawn. They lay eggs in layers and, if the conditions are right, can lay up to 300 eggs in a few hours. These new fish grow to adulthood within nine months.

RESEARCH PROJECT

List three animals that live in the lowland, swampy areas of Singapore. Then research the swampy areas where you live. What different animals live there? List three of them, and then compare and contrast the two lists: how are the animals listed similar and how are they different?

TEXT-DEPENDENT QUESTIONS

1. What are two birds that can be found in Singapore?

2. What is Singapore's highest point?

3. When are Singapore's monsoon seasons?

SINGAPORE'S GEOGRAPHY & LANDSCAPE

Buddha Tooth Relic Temple and Museum is a modern building based on Tang Dynasty architecture. It was built to house a relic of Buddah's tooth.

WORDS TO UNDERSTAND

Sanskrit: a language of ancient India with historical documentation dating back 3,500 years

session: regarding government, a meeting of a deliberative body where it conducts business

surrender: to submit to the authority of an opponent or enemy

CHAPTER 2

THE GOVERNMENT & HISTORY OF SINGAPORE

Singapore's history is not well recorded, which makes it difficult to know much about it before the 1200s. Most of Singapore's known history starts from the fourteenth century. This was the first time the area received the name "Singapura," starting it on the path to become Singapore later in the future.

Singapore's Early History

The earliest records of Singapore date back to the third century when a Chinese account calls it *Pu Luo Chung*, or "The Island at the End of a Peninsula." Later on, the city took on the name *Temasek*, which means "sea town." It was called Temasek when the first known settlements were established in 1292 to 1299 CE.

In the fourteenth century, Singapore received a new name. According to legends, a prince from Palembang, which is the capital of Srivijaya, went on a hunting trip on the island when he saw an animal that he'd never witnessed before. He believed this was a positive sign and renamed the city Singapura, which means "The Lion City." It comes from the **Sanskrit** words for lion, *simha,* and city, *pura.*

Little India in Singapore is a vibrant area of older-style buildings. It is a neighborhood of temples, restaurants, shops, and other interesting places to visit.

Five different kings of ancient Singapura ruled after it was renamed. The area became popular because of its location, which made it the ideal meeting spot for countries trading by sea. A trading post was established that allowed many nations to meet within Singapura's borders.

The Founding of Modern Singapore

In the nineteenth century, modern Singapore was established. This is attributed to a man known as Sir Thomas Stamford Raffles. He was the lieutenant-governor of Bencoolen, which is now Bengkulu, in Sumatra. The British wanted to establish a port of call in the area, and Singapore seemed perfect. Raffles was quickly sent and arrived at Singapore in January 1819. He helped local rulers negotiate a treaty with Sumatra as a trading station, which began to attract immigrants from India, China, the Malay Archipelago, and other locations.

Raffles implemented what is today known as the Raffles Town Plan, or the Jackson Plan, in 1822. This was created to help keep order despite the growing disorganization of the colony. The plan called for separating ethnic residents into one of four areas. The rest of the country's area was then separated into the "European Town," which contained European traders, rich Asians, and Eurasians. Present-day Chinatown is where the Chinese were asked to move. Ethnic Indians moved to Chulia Kampong, north of Chinatown. And Muslims, Arabs, and ethnic

Sir Thomas Stamford Raffles, founder of modern Singapore.

The famous Raffles Hotel opened in 1899. It was named after Singapore's founder.

Malays moved to Kampong Glam as individuals who had migrated to Singapore.

Singapore in World War II

Singapore had been prosperous before World War II, but that came to an end when it was attacked by the Japanese on December 8, 1941. British leaders had expected an attack from the south, where the Japanese could come by sea. Unfortunately, Japan attacked from the north, which caught the British off guard. The battle was lost, and Allied forces **surrendered** on Chinese New Year in 1942.

Once the Japanese surrendered in 1945, the island was given back to the British Military Administration. It retained power until the Straits Settlement was dissolved. Shortly after, Singapore became a British Crown Colony in 1946.

Sir Thomas Stamford Raffles

Sir Thomas Stamford Raffles was the British East Indian administrator and founder of the port city of Singapore. He was a vital component in the creation of Britain's Far Eastern empire, which is largely a result of his contributions. He was knighted in 1816, just three years before establishing Singapore.

Sir Thomas Stamford Raffles grew up in poverty and surrounded by debt. He stopped going to school at fourteen and began working for the East India Company. His formal education did not meet the requirements of the job, but he studied science and numerous languages on his own. He also took an interest in natural history, which earned him a positive, and distinguished, reputation among colleagues. At just twenty-three years of age, he was appointed as the assistant secretary of Penang. He went on to establish the port in Singapore in 1819, and in 1822, he returned to create Singapore's government. After suffering from debilitating headaches for some time, he returned to England in 1824. He assisted in founding the London Zoo before he passed away from a brain tumor in 1826.

The evacuation of British POWs following the Japanese surrender in 1945. Kallang Airport control tower still stands today, opposite the National Stadium.

Singapore's Independence

Nationalism grew steadily in Singapore and by 1959, the country had developed its own government. In its first election, the People's Action Party won, resulting in Lee Kuan Yew taking the position of the first prime minister of Singapore.

Shortly after, in 1963, Malaysia was created. It was made up of Singapore, Sarawak, North Borneo, and the Federation of Malaya. It was not a successful merger for Singapore, and the country left Malaysia in August 1965 to become an independent nation.

THE GOVERNMENT & HISTORY OF SINGAPORE

The Parliament House is where Singapore's government is located.

The Singaporean Government

The government of Singapore comprised of the president and the Cabinet. Although the president is allowed to act at their personal discretion for certain functions his or her role is largely ceremonial. It is the Cabinet, composed of the prime minister and other ministers appointed by the president, that generally directs and controls the government. The cabinet is formed by the political party who wins a majority at a general election. Each parliament lasts for a maximum of five years from the date of its first sitting, and once a parliament has been dissolved a general election must be held within three months.

The government of Singapore is modeled after the British system, called the Westminster System. It has three branches, the Legislative, Executive, and Judiciary. The Legislature is in charge of producing laws. The Executive branch administers the law, and the Judiciary is in charge of interpreting laws. The head of Singapore's government is the prime minister, and the president is the Head of State. The first Cabinet of Singapore was led by Lee Kuan Yew, who was elected as prime minister in 1959.

What makes Singapore's government interesting is that it is unicameral. That means that the Parliament of Singapore has only a single House. The members of the House, called Members of Parliament (MPs), are chosen through general

Choosing the Party Whip

The government "whip" is perhaps not what it sounds like. The Party Whip is actually an important political role—a person who is in charge of communicating within the party and guaranteeing that Parliament runs smoothly. The Whip is in charge of listing the Members of Parliament (MPs) who will be speaking during each item of business during a **session**. The Whip also estimates the time that each person will be allowed to have to be heard and makes sure that the speech is completed on time.

Essentially, the Party Whip is a disciplinarian. This person encourages party members to support their party's position, but there are times when they may also allow them to vote with their conscience. In 2019, the Government Whip is Mr. Chan Chun Sing. He and two Deputy Government Whips work together to keep order in the House.

elections. The leader of the party who is elected is then asked by the president to be established as the prime minister (PM). The PM gets to choose their own ministers from the MPs who were already elected by the people. The MPs whom the PM chooses will form the country's cabinet.

There is also another position available, called the Speaker of Parliament. This speaker is elected when a new Parliament meets for the first time. Each Parliament is only able to run for five years without a new election. This election has to be held three months after the current Parliament will be dissolved.

Singapore's Prime Minister Lee Hsien Loong (right) and Vietnamese Prime Minister Nguyen Xuan Phuc, in 2017.

Today, Singapore is a modern and vibrant city state.

RESEARCH PROJECT

Pick three major events in Singaporean history. Draw a timeline, beginning with its founding (around 1820) and ending with Prime Minister Lee Hsien Loong, who was last elected in 2016. Indicate where your three major events fall on the timeline.

TEXT-DEPENDENT QUESTIONS

1. What is the Singaporean government based on?

2. What is a Party Whip?

3. When did Singapore leave the Federation of Malaya?

THE GOVERNMENT & HISTORY OF SINGAPORE   27

WORDS TO UNDERSTAND

exemption: the process of exempting a person from having to pay taxes; allowing someone not to be taxed for a portion of their earnings

fiscal: related to the government's revenue or taxes

per capita income: the average income per person in a given location during the course of a certain year

SINGAPORE'S ECONOMY

CHAPTER 3

Every country has a unique economy. Singapore's booming economy is second only to Hong Kong, which boasts the freest economy in the world. Singapore has done well despite its size, having been able to create a strong government, a stable economy, and a free-market economy that continues to grow and flourish. Trade is embraced, and international businesses often look to Singapore as a place to invest, to hold meetings, or to send their business.

The Economy of Singapore

Singapore's economic freedom ranking is 2, making it the second freest country in the world in 2019. Its score increased slightly due to improvements in trade freedom and government integrity. There have been some declines in property rights and labor freedom. Singapore is ranked second out of forty-three countries in the Asia-Pacific area.

Singapore ranks high thanks to its exceptional free-market economy and the business environment, which is primarily free of corruption. The government also has an encouraging industrial policy targeting **fiscal** incentives and encouraging development that will attract foreign investment. It focuses on economic

The industrial area of Jurong is in the western part of Singapore.

diversification and public investment, which keep the economy balanced, and entrepreneurship is promoted, too, which boosts the economy on the whole.

Singapore is among the most prosperous nations in the world by **per capita income**. It is usually listed in the top ten of richest countries in the world. Recent figures show that Singapore has a per capita income of $93,905 in international dollars. In comparison, the United States ranked eleventh, with a per capita income of $59,532 (international dollars).

The People's Action Party has been in control of the government for decades, which is what makes it so stable. International trade is embraced by the current government, as is economic liberalization. Singapore controls one of the largest ports on Earth, and it has one of the lowest unemployment rates in the developed world. Singapore relies on exports of refined petroleum, computers, and integrated circuits.

Workers on a sea container vessel.

The Economy of Singapore

Gross Domestic Product (GDP):
$528.1 billion USD

Industries:
electronics, chemicals, financial services, oil drilling equipment, petroleum refining, biomedical products, scientific instruments, telecommunication equipment, processed food and beverages, ship repair, offshore platform construction

Agriculture:
vegetables, poultry, eggs, fish, ornamental fish, orchids

Export Commodities:
machinery and equipment, electronics and telecommunications, pharmaceuticals, chemicals, refined petroleum products, foodstuffs

Export Partners:
China 14.7%, Hong Kong 12.6%, Malaysia 10.8%, US 6.6%, Indonesia 5.8%, Japan 4.7%, South Korea 4.6%, Thailand 4%

Import Commodities:
machinery and equipment, mineral fuels, chemicals, foodstuffs, consumer goods

Import Partners:
China 13.9%, Malaysia 12%, US 10.7%, Japan 6.3%, South Korea 5%

Currency:
Singapore dollar

Source: www.cia.gov 2017

SINGAPORE'S ECONOMY

The import and export of goods is a major part of Singapore's economy. The port of Singapore is the busiest commercial port in Asia.

Taxes and Other Income

Taxes in Singapore are applied differently to residents and nonresidents. You are considered a resident if you are a citizen or permanent resident, or if you have worked or stayed in Singapore for 183 days or longer in the year prior to the tax assessment of the current year.

Residential tax rates:

Income up to 20,000 SGD (US$14,769) is not taxed. On the next 10,000 SGD (US$7,384), there is a tax of 2 percent. The next 10,000 SGD (US$7,384) is taxed at 3.5 percent. A 7 percent tax rate is charged on the next 40,000 SGD (US$29,538), and the following 40,000 SGD (US$29,538) is charged at 11.5 percent. This continues to increase for each additional 40,000 SGD (US$29,538) at rates of 15, 18, 19, 19.5, 20 and 22 percent.

Those who are not residents are tax exempt on income earned within Singapore for 60 days or less in each year, although some limited exceptions do apply to this rule. For days 61 through 182, income earned by nonresidents is taxed at 15 percent or the resident rate, whichever is higher. Consultant fees and directors' fees are taxed at 22 percent.

There is one special tax scheme to know about named the Not Ordinarily Resident Scheme, or NOR. To qualify for NOR status, a person must be a nonresident in the past three years of assessment. In the assessment year in which they first qualify for NOR status, they must then be a Singapore resident. A qualified NOR taxpayer can obtain special tax treatment for five years, only paying income tax on a part of the income earned during the days they're in Singapore. The NOR taxpayer is also able to receive a tax **exemption** on employer contributions to overseas pension funds.

Residents of Singapore pay taxes on a scale according to their pay grade.

The Labor Force

The labor force of most countries is split into three sectors: agriculture, industry, and services. However in Singapore, agriculture doesn't add hardly anything to the country's Gross Domestic Product (GDP). As of 2008, land that was labeled "agriculture" only totaled 3 square miles (8 square kilometers). In a country with so little land, it's too valuable to be used for agriculture.

Industry makes up 24.8 percent of the labor force and services make up 75.2 percent, according to 2017 estimates. Around 3.6 million people are employed in these two economic segments, excluding nonresidents. Split up by occupation, 0.7 percent of people work in agriculture, 25.6 percent work in industry and 73.7 percent work in services. As of 2017, there was an unemployment rate of 2.2 percent.

Singapore's Hospitality Industry

Singapore's hotel industry has an important influence on the economy. Some types of categories of businesses in this industry include the travel industry, hotel industry, food and beverage businesses, entertainment businesses, and tourist attractions. These may include individual services such as flights, trains and buses, rental cars, motels, restaurants, sports, and historical sites.

Altogether, these bring a large amount of money into Singapore, despite the fact that it isn't a large country. The nation is known for its luxurious hotels and foods. There are actually over 400 hotels in Singapore, and more are still being built.

International visitors looking for a place to stay during business meetings, those in search of medical procedures, and those who enjoy gambling support the booming hospitality industry. There was a small dip in visitors in 2016, but the tourism board expects the numbers to continue moving forward, and the country has been investing in new hotels, and even more entertainment venues. MICE, which stands for Meetings, Incentive, Convention and Exhibitions business, is the primary reason for the success of the hospitality industry.

A video explaining some public transportation options in Singapore.

Economic Sectors

The two primary economic sectors in Singapore are industry and services. Only 0.7 percent of the labor force works in agriculture, producing vegetables, eggs, fish, ornamental fish, orchids, and poultry.

The industrial sector is projected to grow by 5.7 percent as of the 2017 estimate. Industries in Singapore include electronics, financial services, ship repair, offshore platform construction, processed food and beverages, telecommunication equipment, biomedical products, petroleum refining, oil drilling equipment, scientific instruments, chemicals, and trade. Most people work in the services sector—tourism, banking, and other necessary services throughout the country.

Transportation

Getting around Singapore could not be easier thanks to its small size and simple

SINGAPORE'S ECONOMY 35

An SBS Transit city bus arriving at a station.

public transportation options. There are three primary types of public transportation in Singapore: Mass Rapid Transit (MRT), buses, and taxis. The most common form of transportation is the bus, which is available in almost every area in Singapore. Since public buses are so readily available, they're recognized as the most extensive form of public transport in the country. The MRT, on the other hand, is known for speed.

Buses

Buses in Singapore are operated by one of two operators—SBS Transit or SMRT. SMRT uses yellow buses, while SBS Transit uses red and white buses. Each company has its own routes and interchanges, so it's important to be aware that not all bus routes connect. Buses run from 5:30 a.m. through midnight, and there are occasional Nite Owl and NightRider services that cost more but extend later into the early morning.

Possibly the best thing about buses in Singapore is that nearly all of them have air conditioning. They also cost very little.

Some feeder buses are available, and they also charge low rates. These buses usually run on smaller circuits and end at major terminals or interchanges.

Singapore's Mass Rapid Transit

The MRT lines from north to south and east to west were started in May 1982, with construction costing $5 billion SGD. Since then, the MRT has been extended, with a line connecting the northern and western stations. A Northeast Line was added to connect Punggol and Sengkang to downtown. Operating from 2010 onward was The Circle Line, which links all radial lines that lead to the city.

The MRT is in good shape thanks to solid construction and regular maintenance. It is very useful for getting from downtown to the outskirts of Singapore and vice versa. Recently, a new system, the Light Rapid Transit (LRT), was added. It has intra-town loop services, so passengers can move from the MRT to the LRT to get to different parts of towns. Right now, the LRT is available in Bukit Panjang, Punggol, and Sengkang housing estates.

The Mass Rapid Transit train is an efficient mode of transport for commuters traveling to the city.

Using Taxis in Singapore

Taxis are also indispensable. There are eight carriers that are presently well known in Singapore: CityCab, Yellow Top Taxi, SMRT Taxis, SMART Automobile, Prime Taxi, Premier Taxi, Trans-Cab Services, and Comfort Transportation. Taxis are used for privacy and more speed, but they can get held up in heavy traffic. The good thing about using a taxi is that most experienced drivers will know which routes to take during congested times of the day or night, so they are able to avoid traffic jams. This is the least economical option, but taxi drivers charge by meter and are fair and transparent with fares.

Energy

Singapore has been working to reduce its greenhouse gas emissions and has turned to using less carbon-intensive fuels. The government looks for ways to make the country more efficient and to reduce the energy use in

The PSTLES Initiative

The Public Sector Taking the Lead in Environmental Sustainability program is a long-term initiative aimed a using Singapore's resources efficiently. This initiative was introduced in 2006 anc encourages people to take seriously the actions involved with water efficiency, recycling, and energy efficiency. The PSTLES program was enhanced in 2014, adding oversight with a Sustainability Manager who set targets to be met by fiscal year 2020. The manager would also assist in developing resource management plans that would meet the targets of the area.

Singapore is still relying on carbon-based fuels for its energy needs. This is an oil refinery on Singapore's coast.

each sector. The three sectors targeted by the government's incentives, public education, and legislation include the household sector, industry sector, and public sector.

Right now, Singapore primarily uses natural gas for energy. It switched to natural gas from fuel oil to reduce its carbon emissions. Of all the different fossil fuel-fired plants, energy created with natural gas emits the least carbon.

The government takes energy use seriously and has rolled out several incentives. For example, the Save Energy Save Money initiative encourages households to practice energy-saving habits. By doing so, they can save money and have the added bonus of helping fight against climate change. This public awareness campaign is also aimed at offices and energy management in the workplace.

    The government has implemented Mandatory Energy Labelling, shortened to MELS, as well as Minimum Energy Performance Standards (MEPS) on appliances for the home. The United States has a similar protocol, requiring home appliance manufacturers to provide an EnergyGuide label that shows the estimated energy usage per year. Household appliances must also state their efficiency ratings in Singapore so people can choose those that use less energy and will lower their energy bills.

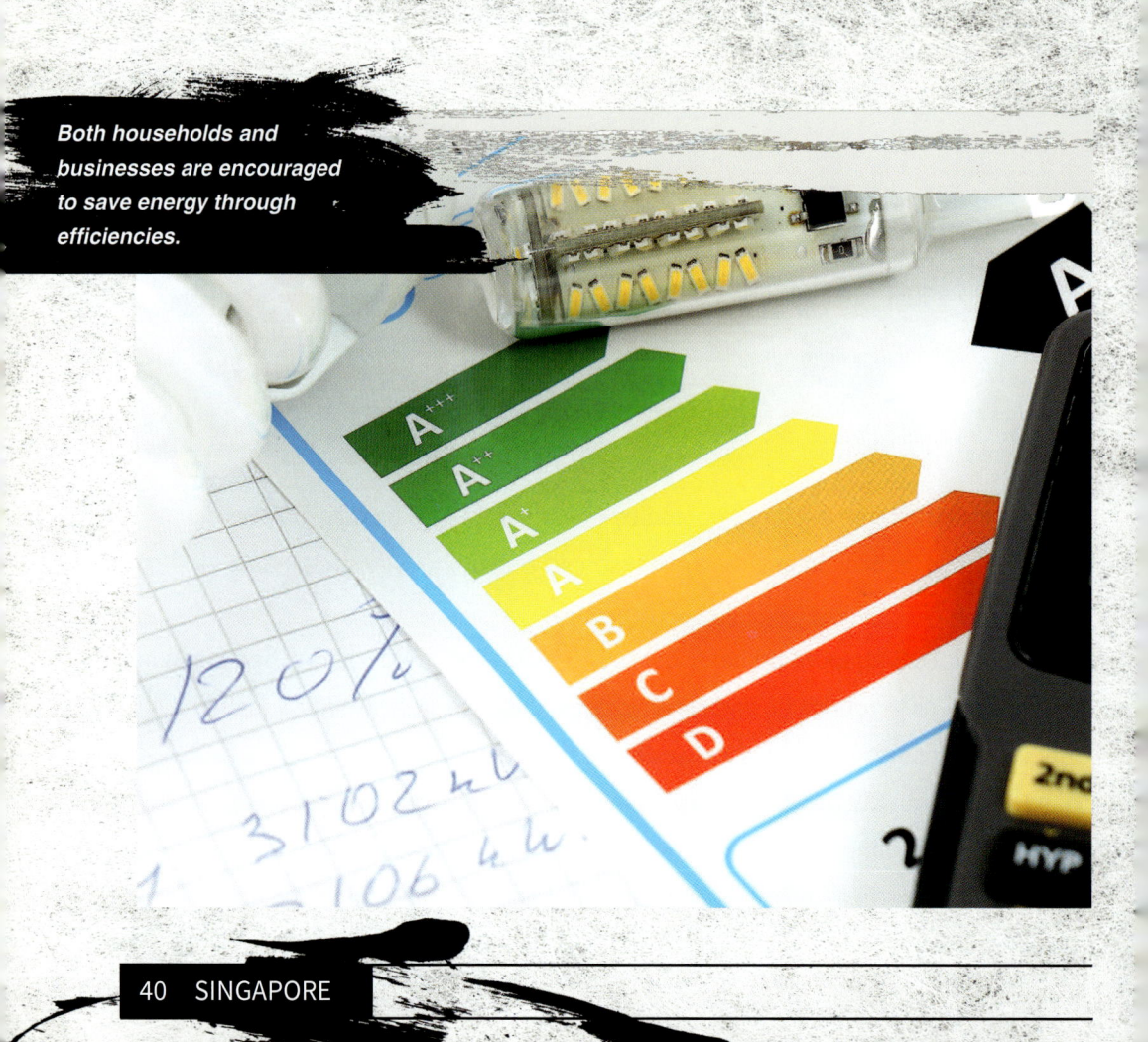

Both households and businesses are encouraged to save energy through efficiencies.

There are more than 7,000 multinational corporations from all over the world based in Singapore.

In the industrial sector, MEPS applies to energy conservation in businesses. There are grants and incentives for businesses, such as the Energy Efficiency Fund and Energy Efficiency Financing Programme.

For the public sector, there is a focus on reducing carbon emissions to help the environment and to lower power costs. The Public Sector Taking the Lead in Environmental Sustainability (PSTLES) program is an initiative to develop better resource efficiency, including energy efficiency, recycling, and water efficiency.

Economic Problems

Singapore has a strong economy as of 2019. However, it does face some challenges in the global environment. Since the economy has grown rapidly in the past, the reality is that it will have to slow eventually. It has some growth

Like many countries in the West, Singapore has an aging population.

opportunities with its placement in the three economic growth areas of ASEAN, as well as India and China. However, changing international competitiveness and economic nationalism could disrupt its potential.

Another problem that plagues Singapore is an aging population, along with a slowing population growth. Rising costs, combined with weak innovation, could also hurt the economy overall.

However, for the most part, the economy of Singapore is in good shape. It's a key hub of Southeast Asia, which means that it is indispensable, and Singapore is also a global destination. It offers business services, is known for its finance industry, and is a robust manufacturing base. On the whole, it's involved in high value-added activities, which means it gets as much as it can out of its agreements with others.

Singapore's financial and business district.

RESEARCH PROJECT

Transportation is important to any community in the world. Discuss how you believe Singapore could improve its transportation in a one-page paper.

TEXT-DEPENDENT QUESTIONS

1. What kinds of initiatives does Singapore have in place to promote better energy usage?

2. What are some economic issues that Singapore could face in the future?

3. What are four kinds of transportation in Singapore?

A diverse group of Singaporean women including Malay, Chinese, and Eurasian.

WORDS TO UNDERSTAND

anarchy: a state of disorder that occurs when citizens ignore or refuse to recognize governmental authority or other controlling systems

assimilate: to be or become absorbed; to conform or adjust to the customs, attitudes, etc., of a group, nation, or the like

geomancy: seeking to discover hidden knowledge or benefits by means of invisible lines created by furniture placement so as to harmonize with the spiritual forces that inhabit it

CITIZENS OF SINGAPORE— PEOPLE, CUSTOMS & CULTURE

CHAPTER 4

Singapore is a multicultural nation, with many ethnicities that have come together to create the nation it is today. Much like the United States, it is a melting pot. However, despite the fact that many people have come to live in this country, their cultures have remained somewhat separate. Certain groups and ethnicities retain their independence from one another, celebrating their own holidays and events. However, on the whole, everyone is welcoming of anyone or anything from another culture and the population works hard to **assimilate** new pieces of culture into the overall Singaporean culture.

To better understand Singapore's culture, you have to look at the ethnicities that make it up. You can then get a better idea of why certain foods, activities, and even education systems are in place today.

Ethnicities

There are a variety of ethnicities in Singapore, with ethnic Chinese making up the majority of the population at 76.2 percent. Malays make up approximately 15 percent of the ethnic population and ethnic Indians make up another 7.4 percent. Malays are recognized as the indigenous people of Singapore.

Singapore has been polyglot and multiethnic since it was founded in 1819, but the Chinese have been in the majority since 1830. Singapore doesn't have a dominant primary culture, so it has always been difficult for immigrants to assimilate, or learn one common language. One thing to note is that the majority of people in Singapore still marry within their ethnic group. Some intermarriages do take place, but gaps in income between ethnic groups have existed for a long time and separates the group socially.

The educational system in Singapore encourages pupils to fulfill their true potential.

Here is a short video exploring Singapore's twenty-first century approach to teaching.

Education

Education is taken seriously in Singapore and students aim for excellence. Families have the choice of preschools, primary schools, secondary school, and post-secondary education. The school systems in Singapore have a positive reputation among families, as well as internationally.

Parents who want to enroll their children in school have to register around a year in advance. Then they can attend preschool, move on to kindergarten, junior colleges, and any other academic interests their children may have.

In Singapore, the secondary school that children attend will determine their careers in the future. For example, those who achieve A levels move on to university, while those who do not may go to technical institutes for training.

The education system believes in developing children's skills and strengths, and social skills are encouraged. Overall, Singapore's students do well and pursue

Singaporeans love soccer. This group is practicing their skills.

excellent careers. The government spends time reforming the educational system, continuing to improve it. Many nations look to Singapore for answers on how to make their educational systems better for the future.

Sports

Some of the most popular recreational sports in Singapore include soccer, basketball, swimming, cricket, and sailing.

Since Singapore is an island nation, water sports are particularly popular. Waterskiing, kayaking and sailing are sports participated in often.

Singaporeans are fond of soccer, and their national team won the Tiger Cup championships in 1998, 2004, 2007, and 2012.

Singapore has won several Olympic Games medals, including a 1960 silver medal won by Tan Howe Liang in weightlifting. The first time a gold medal was won was in 2016, thanks to swimmer Joseph Schooling. Li Jiawei, Feng Tianwei, and Wang Yuegu also won a silver medal in women's double table tennis in 2008's Beijing Summer Olympics. In the 2002 Asian Games, Singapore triumphed with seventeen medals: five gold, two silver, and ten bronze.

Joseph Schooling receiving a gold medal in swimming at the Rio Olympic Games in 2016.

CITIZENS OF SINGAPORE—PEOPLE, CUSTOMS & CULTURE

Language

Several languages are commonly used in Singapore: Malay, English, Tamil, Mandarin Chinese, and Standard Mandarin. Most Singaporeans are bilingual because the country has a dual-language learning system. Since the 1960s, it has been compulsory for students in primary schools to learn a second language. It has been compulsory in secondary schools since 1966, and the Ministry of Education continues to encourage the policy.

Today, basic educational materials are printed and taught in English. In addition, most children learn at least one of the three other primary languages, with Malay being the chief language encouraged by the government. Most children learn the language that corresponds with their official registered ethnic group. If their parents intermarried and they have a hyphenated race, then the first race is what is used to determine the second language.

Young Singaporeans are encouraged to learn a second language.

Kopi-O is a type of black coffee that is popular with Singaporeans.

Many older texts and pieces of literature exist in Singapore that were written in multiple languages. If students or residents want to read them, they need to be bilingual, trilingual, or multilingual. Being able to speak multiple languages is a huge benefit to those in Singapore, so it is not uncommon to see people who speak two, three, or more languages. Scientists who have studied multilingual people have learned that the practice enhances a person's ability to store and process information, giving them a better working memory.

Even Singaporean English is not quite the same as English in the United States, just like English in Canada or the United Kingdom may vary. In fact, Singaporean English is a combination of Mandarin, Tamil, and other languages, creating unique slang and interesting phrasing.

Singaporean Drinks

There are many unique drinks found in Singapore including Kopi-O, Milo Dinosaur, bandung, bubble tea, sugarcane juice, tiger beer, and chin chow drink. There are so many unique beverages that it would be impossible to name them all, but these are among the most popular.

Kopi-O, for instance, is a type of black coffee with sugar. It's called "Kopi Tiam" within Singapore. It has a high caffeine content, so it's very popular for early risers.

Another drink, Teh Tarik, is tea liquor combined with milk. It is sweet and is often used to relieve common colds and coughs. Teh Tarik is interesting to see being made, since tea hawkers rapidly move it from one pot to another to make it froth.

With the clever name "Milo Dinosaur," this children's drink is made of Milo, a chocolate malt powder, and cold milk.

Combining cold milk and rose syrup is how bandung is made. It comes in a bubblegum-pink color and it's a welcome drink frequently served at wedding ceremonies.

Feng Shui

Feng shui is also known as Chinese **geomancy**. The practice essentially states that our homes and environments are mirrors of what is happening inside us and need to align with who we are internally, as well as where we'd like to go or how we'd like to grow. In short, the goal is to harmonize your body with your surroundings.

Feng shui literally translates to "wind water." Both wind and water are associated with good health, which is where the name comes from in Chinese. It's believed that feng shui dates back at least 6,000 years. It is related to the way Taoists understand nature, which is that all things are filled with chi, or energy.

To simplify feng shui, consider it the art of placement. Understanding how the placement of objects within a space and the spiritual forces that inhabit it affect you is vital to this practice. To use feng shui in the home, you must be cautious about how you bring in furniture and how you arrange objects. In feng shui, everything in your home has energy, and you want to guide that energy in a way that allows it to flow freely. Doing this brings good luck and fortune to those living in the space.

Another famous drink is sugarcane juice, which became popular because of Singapore's ideal sugarcane-growing environment.

In alcoholic drinks, tiger beer, also called tiger brew, is among the most desired. This domestically brewed drink is sold in around sixty countries and is well respected in Singapore. It's common in bars and retailers.

Finally, there is chin chow drink, also known as Grass Jelly drink. To make it, grass jelly is mixed with water, syrup, fruit crush, and cold milk.

Singaporean Food

Singaporean cuisine is wonderfully diverse as it uses ingredients derived from its many ethnic groups. This combined with its maritime history and important seaport, has resulted in a complex and sophisticated cuisine. The native Malays, the largest

Street food in Singapore is popular with locals and tourists alike. It is a mixture of many cooking styles including Chinese and Indian.

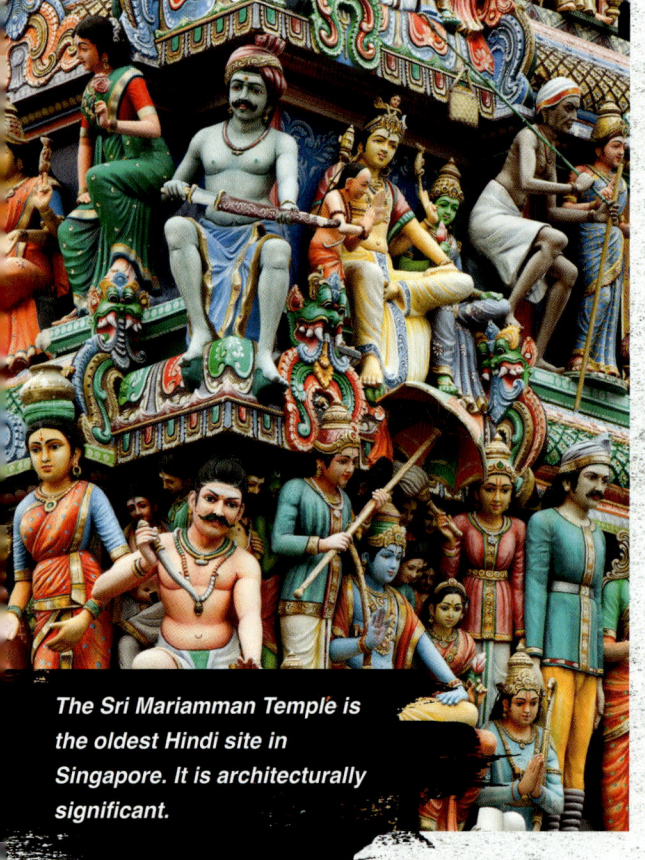

ethnic group; the Chinese; and the third largest ethnic group, the Indians as well as the Indonesians, Peranakan English, and the Portuguese-influenced Eurasians, have all played their parts. Cultures from other regions, migrating to Singapore such as Sri Lankans, Thais, and Middle East people have also influenced the food.

Religion in Singapore

As you may have surmised, Singapore is religiously diverse. Despite its small size, this multicultural country has no specific required or encouraged religion. Singapore's Constitution grants freedom of religion, much like the Constitution of the United States, although the government has banned a few religions. There are also some limitations to religious freedom, however, in that the Constitution prevents religious speech or actions that it decides could adversely affect racial or religious harmony.

The Sri Mariamman Temple is the oldest Hindi site in Singapore. It is architecturally significant.

Some of the religions you can find in Singapore include: Buddhism, Taoism, Christianity, Hinduism, and Islam.

The most prominent of these religions is Buddhism, and most people follow the Mahayana branch. There are also followers of the Theravada school in Singapore. For the most part, those in Singapore who practice Buddhism have a Chinese heritage. Feng Shui is common among Buddhists in Singapore, and Buddhists have strong links to Confucianism and Taoism as well. Many who practice Buddhism are vegetarian.

Islam is also common in Singapore, with most who practice it being Malay. There is an Indian community as well, however. The branch of Islam most practiced in Singapore is Sunni.

Hinduism is practiced in Singapore as well, with most Hindus being from the Indian community. Sri Mariamman Temple is the oldest Hindu temple in Singapore.

Like many other nations, Christianity has a home in Singapore as well. It's usually practiced by the Chinese or Indian people. Different denominations call Singapore home, with the Armenian Church being the oldest Christian church in the country.

Finally, Taoism is the fifth religion you're most likely to see in Singapore. People who practice Taoism are generally Chinese, and they practice the teachings of Lao Tzu. Harmony through Yin Yang comes from Taoism directly. The Taoist temple, Thian Hock Keng, is located in Singapore.

The Armenian Church of Saint Gregory is the oldest Christian church in Singapore.

CITIZENS OF SINGAPORE—PEOPLE, CUSTOMS & CULTURE

The Singapore Art Museum is housed in a restored nineteenth century mission school. It was the first fully dedicated visual arts museum in Singapore.

The Arts: Architecture, Painting, Music, and Literature

Singapore has an unusual and unique art scene in that it includes a great number of different styles. Many countries have contributed to its growth, and so the arts include paintings, dances, music, theater, and sculpture among other arts. Artistic creation often mixes classic European styles with symbolism from Asia.

    Chinese culture has influenced the art of Singapore significantly. For example, Chinese calligraphy, sculptures, and porcelain all affected Singapore's art scene.

    One of the most famous places to view art in Singapore is the Singapore National Gallery, where works from notable artists are on display for the world to see. Singapore holds several festivals over the course of a year that celebrate the arts and encourage international exhibitions.

Singapore's contemporary art scene emerged in the 1970s, as multiculturalism became mainstream. The first art gallery was only established after World War II, despite the fact that museums have been in the country for over 100 years. Historians believe that Singapore's art scene emerged from the evolution of its own people and the country's history, not in conjunction with international trends in art.

Singapore commercializes some of its arts, but this was not common until after the first art exhibition in 1950, staged by the Singapore Art Society. In the 1980s, more artists emerged, particularly those working in mixed media, which was in sharp contrast to the watercolor paintings of the Nanyang style (a style of painting practiced by migrant Chinese painters in Singapore in the 1950s).

Malay Girls *by Singaporean artist Chen Wen Hsi. It is from a collection housed in the Singapore Art Museum.*

The Flower Dome and the Cloud Forest is situated in Singapore's Gardens by the Bay. It is a fascinating place to visit and architecturally important.

Painting

Paintings in Singapore were greatly influenced by Nanyang art. Oftentimes, artists used techniques from China but applied their use to different cultures. European influences are often seen in Nanyang art, along with influences from indigenous religious beliefs and cultural heritage. Some notable Nanyang artists include Georgette Chen and Chen Wen Hsi. Modern art in Singapore, from the twentieth century onward, does not mean quite the same thing as it does in the United States. Singapore's modern art has been most concerned with representing local, indigenous identities through art.

Although painting is a relatively modern artistic endeavor throughout Singapore, international influences can be seen. When Singapore holds art exhibitions and festivals, it's common to see artists from around the globe flock to the cities to showcase their work.

Architecture

Architecture in Singapore is a combination of colonial buildings, heritage sites, and cutting-edge structures. The Design Director of the Ministry of Design, Colin Seah, has stated that Singaporean architecture serves as milestones: manifestations of the country's dreams and aspirations.

Like in other areas of the arts, architecture has been influenced by cultures from around the world. From Malay homes to colonial structures, almost any type of structure can be found in Singapore. There are many European influences including Renaissance, Palladian, Gothic and Neoclassical styles.

The ArtScience Museum is located within the resort of Marina Bay Sands in the downtown area of Singapore.

A view of the Oasia Hotel with its living tower. This is Singapore's way to bring nature to high-rise urban areas.

One unique thing you'll see in Singapore is an array of stepped gardens and roof gardens. Because of the lack of green space due to limited land area, many architects try to combine nature with homesteads, adding literal forests to the tops of skyscrapers and greenery around homes with cascading planters. Modern design is mixed in with the classical architecture of the past, creating space-age structures that take into consideration the human need for green spaces.

One example of mixing nature and commercialism is WOHA's Oasia Hotel, which is a living green tower. Aluminum mesh paneling was attached along its sides, which allows twenty-one species of creepers, flowers, and plants to grow up the side of the skyscraper. They help improve air quality in the city and provide a level of natural air conditioning by shading the building's occupants from the sun, as well as providing homes for wildlife.

Music

There is a lack of historical documentation on music in Singapore, which is why it's difficult to know exactly how it developed. What can be said is that the music of Singapore now reflects a multicultural society. It was obviously influenced by the West, particularly when looking at some of the first documented music in the 1950s—jazz and swing. In the 1960s, the development of bands with lead singers, three guitarists, a drummer, and keyboardist became popular and led to Singapore bands forming. Some include Naomi & The Boys, and The Quests, which is considered the most successful Singaporean band of the 1960s.

By the 1970s, rock 'n' roll had been developed, but Singapore's government determined that the popular event called "tea dances," which had become the focus

Street musicians celebrate the Mid Autumn Festival in Singapore's China Town.

Popular music and culture in Singapore is heavily influenced by the West.

of rock 'n' roll music, were sources of social disorder. In 1973, Defense Minister Goh Keng Swee called Western influences "poisonous." As a result, rock 'n' roll became somewhat of an enemy of the state.

Following this development, many individuals in the 1980s began to feel overly restricted and regulated by the government. This same period overlapped in the UK with the rise of a youth movement that was interested in promoting **anarchy,** and a new musical form called "punk rock."

MTV hit the scene in Singapore, as well as many other countries, shortly thereafter. Sadly, Singapore's musicians saw their efforts overshadowed by international acts and their popularity and influence were reduced.

Today, there are not as many Singaporean acts as you would expect, which is likely still a result of the slow growth in music Singapore saw starting in the 1990s.

Since 2010, thanks to the internet, more Singaporean musicians are breaking into the international scene. Being able to connect on an international stage is the right step for Singapore to take part in the international music scene.

Literature

Literature in Singapore is typically written in English, Standard Mandarin, Tamil, and Malay. The country's literary history is uniquely multilingual. A literary pioneer in the 1800s, Makadoom Saiboo admitted in a short story that success relied on a writer being fluent in Chinese, Malay, Javanese, Bugis, Tamil, Hindi, English, Spanish, and many other languages. The reality is that knowing as many languages as possible can be a significant help to writers, but only four languages have been officially adopted by the government.

Book shops in Singapore stock books in all languages including English.

Several Tamil writers live in Singapore. One, Kanagalatha (Latha), is known for her short stories and poems. She won the 2008 Singapore Literature Prize with a short story, *Women I Murder*.

Chinese literature is also common in Singapore. Many Singaporean novelists, short story writers, and poets choose to write in Mandarin Chinese. One such writer is Yeng Pway Ngon, who won the Singapore Literature Prize three times and also won the Cultural Medallion for Literature.

Singapore has a relatively short history in literature as recorded historically. Most literature is from after the 1800s. But keep in mind that Singapore's multicultural history means that it has many literary pieces from around the globe influencing its people and filling its libraries. It wasn't uncommon to see Indian literature, for example, in certain parts of the country, just as it is not uncommon to see religious texts from various religions on bookshelves.

A branch of the National Library in Orchard Road.

The population of Singapore is incredibly diverse, so therefore its culture is also.

RESEARCH PROJECT

Create a short presentation about Singapore's ethnic groups.

TEXT-DEPENDENT QUESTIONS

1. Why is education considered to be so important in Singapore?

2. What was the first style of painting in Singapore?

3. How is Singapore's architecture unique?

Twin pagodas in the Chinese Garden by The Jurong Lake in Jurong East.

WORDS TO UNDERSTAND

bordering: adjacent to

planned: controlling the development of an area, or creating a layout for the physical characteristics of a town or city

region: an area or division of an area that has distinctive characteristics

FAMOUS CITIES OF SINGAPORE

CHAPTER 5

There are many famous cities in Singapore, and people often travel to see all of them in a single visit thanks to the ease of getting around the country and the country's small size. Since it takes only a few hours to get from one end of Singapore to the other, it's no surprise that tourists often stop by multiple cities before heading out.

Singapore has many populated cities, but these are five that have become well known internationally and that have something to offer tourists who would like to visit.

Jurong East

This town in Singapore is well known for its MRT line. It is in the western **region** of Singapore, **bordering** Jurong West and Boon Lay. Clementi is located to the east of this town, while Bukit Batok and Tengah are to the north. South of the city lies Selat Jurong.

Jurong East is a **planned** area and residential town. It may be better explained as a district of Singapore. It's normal to find residences as well as industrial complexes in this region. The area is vibrant and slated to become suburban once finished. IMM, a mega factory outlet, is located in Jurong East. Visitors may also come here to explore JEM and Jcube, as well as to go to Ng Teng Fong General Hospital.

A city view of Jurong East. It is a modern city with many apartment blocks and formal gardens.

Diners and shoppers visit the popular food stalls at the Clementi 448 Market and Food Centre.

It is easy to reach Jurong East since it is on the MRT line. Once there, travelers may like to explore the Jurong Bird Park or Singapore Science Centre. The famous Chinese and Japanese Gardens are located in Jurong East, too.

Clementi

Clementi is another planned area and residential town within Singapore, located in the west. There are many things to do in Clementi, including visiting Clementi Mall. It

FAMOUS CITIES OF SINGAPORE

Pasir Ris Park is located alongside a beach in the eastern part of Singapore.

is adjacent to the Clementi MRT station, making it easy to get to from almost anywhere in Singapore. For visitors eager to view local temples, Ang Chee Sia Ong Temple is one to visit in Clementi. Darussalam Mosque is also located within the town, providing a location for prayer and events in the Islamic community. For those interested in natural history, the Lee Kong Chian Natural History Museum shouldn't be missed.

A short video exploring the Chinese gardens in Singapore.

For spectacular views of the town and the natural world around it, travelers should visit the Southern Ridges. A series of bridges connect Mount Faber Park, Kent Ridge Park, and Telok Blangah Hill Park.

Pasir Ris

Located in the eastern region of Singapore, Pasir Ris is a residential town with many beaches along its border, which is why it is a popular tourist destination. One fun place to go is Pasir Ris Park, which is a beach park that opened in 1989. It's one of the largest in Singapore and covers around 173 acres (70 hectares) of land, making the park, in total, around 4 miles (6.5 kilometers) long. The park is split into sections, and people who love camping can stay overnight in Areas 1 and 3. There is a 15-acre (6-hectare) mangrove forest in the park, with many boardwalks where visitors can explore. It's also popular to participate in bird watching.

FAMOUS CITIES OF SINGAPORE   71

The park isn't the only fun thing to do in Pasir Ris. There is also the White Sands shopping center, theme parks, and bowling alleys.

Pasir Ris is part of a plan to develop wafer fabrication (semiconductor processing) facilities in Singapore. Pasir Ris also has two recycling facilities.

Kampong Glam

Kampong Glam is a neighborhood within Singapore that is well known for its uniqueness. The eclectic area has a blend of historical venues, cultural exploration options, and a trendy lifestyle scene. The popular landmark, Sultan Mosque, is located in Kampong Glam.

Kampong Glam is Singapore's oldest urban quarter. Its name comes from Malay, in which Kampong means "compound." Glam refers to *gelam*, a long-leaved paperbark tree, but locals now use the more common definition, "glamorous."

Sultan Mosque

The Sultan Mosque is also known as "Masjid Sultan." It is located in Kampong Glam and is the primary point where the Muslim community meets in Singapore. It was built in 1824 for Sultan Hussein Shah, who was the first Sultan of Singapore. Sir Stamford Raffles gave Kampong Glam to the sultan, and Temenggong, along with an annual stipend. The sultan built a palace in the city and brought his family and entourage from the Riau islands. Most of his followers came to Singapore and Kampong Glam from Sumatra and Malacca. The mosque was built between 1824 and 1826 with funds from the East India Company. It had a two-tier pyramidal roof at the time of its construction. Sultan Mosque became too small for the community of Muslims in Singapore by 1924, and the trustees approved a plan to create a new mosque in its place. The new mosque, Sultan Mosque, was completed in 1932 and has remained relatively unchanged since that date, except an annex was added in 1993.

Sir Thomas Stamford Raffles established Kampong Glam as an area for the Malay, Bugis, and Arab communities in 1822. As a result, the area became a seat of Malay royalty in Singapore.

Kampong Glam is home to the Malay Heritage Centre, Haji Lane, and exciting night markets.

A Kampong Glam shopping area with the Sultan Mosque in the background.

FAMOUS CITIES OF SINGAPORE 73

Bukit Batok is a large residential district located along the eastern boundary of the West Region of Singapore.

Bukit Batok

Bukit Batok is a mature residential town located in the West Region of Singapore. It is the 25th largest city in the country. Interestingly, the city is built on Gombak norite, which is a geological formation. This allowed the city to have a booming quarrying industry throughout the mid-twentieth century. Throughout the town's six subzones are many notable structures, including the Millennia Institute, Bukit Batok MRT Station, the West Mall, Old Ford Motor Factory, Bukit Batok Nature Park, and Hillview MRT Station.

Burkit Batok Nature Park.

RESEARCH PROJECT

Tourism is a major part of life in Singapore. Explore some possible experiences you could have in two of the cities discussed above and explain why you'd like to travel to these important tourist destinations in a one-page research paper.

TEXT-DEPENDENT QUESTIONS

1. Where can you find the Sultan Mosque?

2. What does the name "Kampong Glam" really stand for?

3. Which city benefitted from the quarrying industry?

Singapore is the world's busiest port in terms of total shipping tonnage. It processes a fifth of the world's shipping containers.

WORDS TO UNDERSTAND

entrepôt: a city or port where goods are brought in for import or sent out for export, collection, and distribution

hydroelectricity: refers to the electricity that is generated by hydropower: the production of electrical power by using the gravitational force of flowing or falling water

intermediary: a person who is a link between people; in conflicts, this person is often referred to as a "mediator"

A BRIGHT FUTURE FOR SINGAPORE

CHAPTER 6

Singapore's Economy

Singapore's economy is ranked as the most open in the world. It is the most pro-business nation and has low tax rates. It ranks third in the world for per capita Gross Domestic Product (GDP) when looking at the country's purchasing power parity (PPP). APEC, the Asia-Pacific Economic Cooperation, is located in Singapore.

Singapore's strong exports in electronics and chemicals, when combined with its position as a regional hub for wealth management, keep it financially secure enough to purchase any natural resources it needed. Because the country is very small, it is unable to produce some of the raw goods needs. As a result, imports are a necessity in the everyday lives of people in Singapore.

As fresh water, land, and other natural resources are scarce in Singapore, the country's economy has grown to rely on **intermediary** trade. This means that it purchases raw goods, refines them, and sells them to others. All goods leaving and arriving are processed though Singapore's **entrepôt**.

Singapore is committed to using renewable energy.

Renewable Energy in Singapore

Renewable energy is energy produced from natural resources that are able to be replenished time and time again, but they have to be available in large quantities in order to be used. In most cases, these resources include **hydroelectricity**, geothermal, wind, and solar energy. Singapore has limited options for renewable energy. Why? Because it's extremely small, there are no hydro resources, and the wind speeds are low. Geothermal energy, produced by the Earth itself, isn't economically viable in Singapore. That means that the only true available renewable resource is solar energy.

Singapore is located in the tropical sun belt and receives the thousands of hours of sunshine that would be necessary for a successful solar-powered nation. Presently, solar power is not commercially viable, but that doesn't mean that it isn't used in some places.

The government has launched the SolarNova Initiative to determine public demand. Additionally, research and development into solar power is being performed to see which solutions could be best for the country while maintaining the stability and reliability of the current energy grid.

Culture Budget

Singapore's revised fiscal year 2017 totals for the Ministry of Culture, Community, and Youth was estimated at $2.09 billion. That was an increase of 7.2 percent from the year before. Out of these funds, 76.3 percent goes to operating expenses and

23.7 percent goes into development. The rise in funding is due to the demand for community sports and the High Performance Sports System.

There are several programs that take place in Singapore under the Ministry of Culture, Community, and Youth:
- The National Arts Council Programme
- The Arts and Heritage Programme
- The Community Relations and Engagement Programme
- The National Youth Council Programme
- The National Heritage Board Programme

Each of these has a different purpose. For example, the National Arts Council Programme contributes to the long-term goals of the arts and culture sector of the

Visitors inside the ArtScience Museum.

country. It funds the School of the Arts, the National Gallery Singapore, The Esplanade Company Limited, and the Singapore Art Museum, to name a few.

The National Arts Council Programme provides money to strengthen the arts ecosystem. This means that the program provides grants, arts housing, and other benefits.

The National Heritage Board Programme educates and works to build up the nation. It is in charge of celebrating shared heritages and is tasked with protecting cultural heritage, broadening access to museums, and participating in archaeology.

The National Youth Council Programme is in charge of two programs, Outward Bound Singapore and Youth Corps Singapore.

The Community Relations and Engagement Programme funds self-help groups and the Tertiary Tuition Fee Scheme for Malay students.

Singapore Today and into the Future

Singapore is currently among the top nations in terms of its economic freedom. However, economists believe that its future may not be as bright as its present. One issue is that aging demographics and rising labor costs will significantly impact the country. Along with many other Asian nations, Singapore relies on the services sector more and more to produce growth. Singapore's manufacturing industry faces strong competition and is at risk from labor costs that keep increasing.

It's believed that Singapore will continue to see modest growth in the manufacturing sector through 2022, and then it will level off and stay in line with world trade at a growth rate of around 2.5 percent yearly.

There are some positives in Singapore too. For instance, the government has a strong desire to invest in and research cutting-edge technology, and there is always a potential to increase the share of exports being sent to neighbors throughout the region. These two factors have kept Singapore's economy stable in the past and likely will continue to do so.

Singapore is a prosperous country that continues to grow—good news for its citizens.

RESEARCH PROJECT

Discuss solar power and why its implementation could be a great benefit to Singapore in a short presentation.

TEXT-DEPENDENT QUESTIONS

1. What are two problems with Singapore's economy?

2. What is the role of the National Heritage Board Programme?

3. What kinds of renewable energy can Singapore benefit from?

A BRIGHT FUTURE FOR SINGAPORE 81

SINGAPOREAN FOOD

People who love food love Singapore. There are so many different kinds of food in Singapore that it would be hard to imagine someone not being able to find something that they can eat there.

Singaporean food is based on diversity. There has always been a large immigrant population in Singapore, which is why it is common to find foods from around the world. Influences most prominent include those from Thailand, the Middle East, Sri Lanka, and the Portuguese. Literature in the country describes eating as a national pastime, making food out to be an obsession around the country. This is somewhat true in that food is a common topic in conversation.

Certain groups in Singapore have strict dietary requirements: Muslims do not eat pork, vegans and vegetarians will not eat most meats or animals, and Hindus do not eat beef.

Thanks to the varied diets of ethnic groups throughout Singapore, it's a great place to travel for people to explore new dietary options. For example, those who are vegan or vegetarian may love that they can mix easily with other vegans or vegetarians in Singapore, where being vegan or vegetarian has become commonplace.

Chili Crab

Makes 2 servings

Ingredients

1 whole cooked crab (about 2 pounds)
2 tbsp flavorless oil
3 garlic cloves, very finely chopped
thumb-sized piece ginger very finely chopped
3 red chilies, 2 very finely chopped, 1 sliced
4 tbsp tomato ketchup
2 tbsp soy sauce
handful cilantro leaves, roughly chopped
2 scallions, sliced
Steamed rice to serve or bao buns

Directions

1. The crab must be prepared before stir-frying (you can ask your fishmonger to do this). This involves removing the claws, the main shell, discarding the inedible parts, then cutting the body into four pieces, and cracking the claws and the legs so the sauce can get through to the meat.

2. Heat the oil in a large wok and sizzle the garlic, ginger, and chopped chilies for 1 minute or until fragrant. Add the ketchup, soy, and 3 ½ fl oz water, and stir to combine. Throw in the crab, turn up the heat and stir-fry for 3-5 mins or until the crab is piping hot and coated in the sauce. Stir through most of the cilantro, scallions, and sliced chili.

3. Use tongs to arrange the crab on a serving dish, pour over the sauce from the pan and scatter over the remaining cilantro, scallions, and sliced chili. Serve with rice or bao buns, and a lot of napkins.

SINGAPOREAN FOOD 83

Singapore Noodles
Makes 4

Ingredients
3 tbsp teriyaki sauce
½ tsp Chinese five-spice powder
2 tsp medium Madras curry powder
11 oz pork tenderloin, trimmed of any fat
5 oz medium egg noodle
1 tbsp sunflower oil
2 x 10 oz packages fresh mixed stir-fry vegetables
3 ½ oz cooked shrimp, thawed if frozen

Directions
1. Mix the teriyaki sauce, five-spice, and curry powders. Add half to the pork, turning to coat, and leave to marinate for 15 minutes.

2. Heat oven to 350 degrees Fahrenheit. Remove pork from the marinade and put on a small baking tray lined with foil. Roast for 15-20 minutes.

3. Meanwhile, cook the noodles following package instructions, but reduce the cooking time by 1 minute. Refresh in cold water and drain very well.

4. Transfer the pork to a chopping board and rest for 5 minutes. Set a large non-stick frying pan or wok over a medium-high heat. Add the oil and stir-fry the vegetables for 3-4 minutes. Cut the pork in half lengthways, then thinly slice. Tip into the pan, with the shrimp, noodles, and remaining marinade. Toss together for 2-3 mins until hot.

SINGAPOREAN FOOD 85

FESTIVALS & HOLIDAYS

If there is one thing Singapore is not, it is not afraid to celebrate cultures from around the globe. Singapore celebrates a variety of holidays from various religions, as well as its own national holidays. People have fun together regardless of their differences, which is one thing that makes Singapore so special internationally.

There are ten official public holidays in Singapore. Since the country is a melting pot of cultures, it's not surprising that some holidays span various religions and come from different parts of the world. The ten recognized holidays celebrated in Singapore are:

- **New Year's Day**
- **Chinese New Year**
- **Good Friday**
- **Labor Day**
- **Vesak Day**
- **National Day**
- **Hari Raya Puasa**
- **Deepavali**
- **Hari Raya Haji**
- **Christmas Day**

Again, these are just the recognized holidays that people get to take off work for. There are many other celebrations that take place within individual communities and among those who are of different backgrounds than what is listed above.

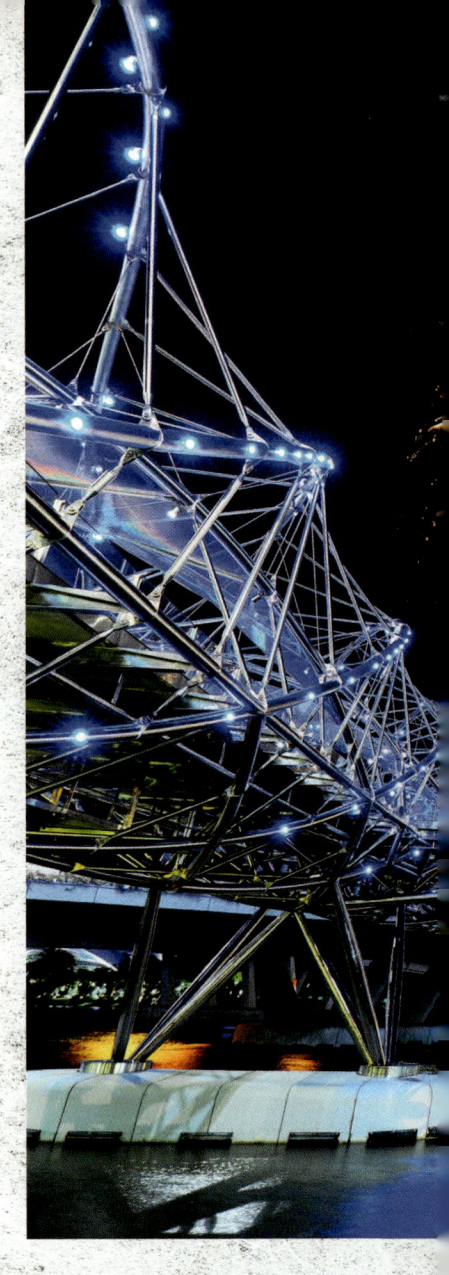

National Day celebrations in Singapore.

There are also festivals and events that are not necessarily linked to religious affiliation or particular cultures outside Singapore. They are not considered national holidays and typically do not result in businesses shutting down or people getting time off work. These include: Singapore Food Festival, Singapore International Film Festival, The Great Singapore Sale, Singapore Fashion Festival, M1 Singapore Fringe Festival, Dragon Boat Festival, and Singapore International Arts Festival.

Series Glossary of Key Terms

aboriginal	Of or relating to the original people living in a region.
archaeology	A science that deals with past human life and activities as shown by objects (as pottery, tools, and statues) left by ancient peoples.
archipelago	A group of islands.
biomass	A renewable energy source from living or recently living plant and animal materials, which can be used as fuel.
Borneo	An island of the Malay Archipelago southwest of the Philippines and divided between Brunei, Malaysia, and Indonesia.
boundary	Something that indicates or fixes a limit or extent.
Buddhism	A religion of eastern and central Asia based on the teachings of Gautama Buddha.
Christianity	A religion based on the teachings of Jesus Christ.
civilization	An advanced stage (as in art, science, and government) in the development of society.
colony	A distant territory belonging to or under the control of a nation.
commodity	Something produced by agriculture, mining, or manufacture.
Confucianism	Of or relating to the Chinese philosopher Confucius or his teachings or followers.
culture	The habits, beliefs, and traditions of a particular people, place, or time.
dialect	A form of a language that is spoken in a certain region or by a certain group.
diversity	The condition or fact of being different.
economic boom	A period of increased commercial activity within either a business, market, industry, or economy as a whole.
emerging market	An emerging market economy is a nation's economy that is progressing toward becoming advanced.
endangered species	A species threatened with extinction.
enterprise	A business organization or activity.
European Union	An economic, scientific, and political organization consisting of 27 European countries.
foreign exchange reserve	Foreign currency reserves that are held by the central bank of a country.
geothermal energy	Energy stored in the form of heat beneath the earth's surface. It is a carbon-free, renewable, and sustainable form of energy.
global warming	A warming of the earth's atmosphere and oceans that is thought to be a result of air pollution.

Hindu	A person who follows Hinduism.
independence	The quality or state of not being under the control of, reliant on, or connected with someone or something else.
industrialization	The widespread development of industries in a region, country, or culture.
infrastructure	The system of public works of a country, state, or region.
interest rate	The proportion of a loan that is charged as interest to the borrower, typically expressed as an annual percentage of the loan outstanding.
Islam	The religious faith of Muslims including belief in Allah as the sole deity and in Muhammad as his prophet.
land reclamation	The process of creating new land from oceans, riverbeds, or lake beds.
landmass	A large area of land.
Malay	A member of a people of the Malay Peninsula, eastern Sumatra, parts of Borneo, and some adjacent islands.
Mandarin	The chief dialect of China.
maritime	Of or relating to ocean navigation or trade.
Mongol	A member of any of a group of traditionally pastoral peoples of Mongolia.
monsoon	The rainy season that occurs in southern Asia in the summer.
mortality rate	The number of a particular group who die each year.
natural resource	Something (as water, a mineral, forest, or kind of animal) that is found in nature and is valuable to humans.
peninsula	A piece of land extending out into a body of water.
precipitation	Water that falls to the earth as hail, mist, rain, sleet, or snow.
recession	A period of reduced business activity.
republic	A country with elected representatives and an elected chief of state who is not a monarch and who is usually a president.
Ring of Fire	Belt of volcanoes and frequent seismic activity nearly encircling the Pacific Ocean.
Shintoism	The indigenous religion of Japan.
street food	Prepared or cooked food sold by vendors in a street or other public location for immediate consumption.
sultan	A ruler especially of a Muslim state.
Taoism	A religion developed from Taoist philosophy and folk and Buddhist religion and concerned with obtaining long life and good fortune often by magical means.
tiger economy	A tiger economy is a nickname given to several booming economies in Southeast Asia.
typhoon	A hurricane occurring especially in the region of the Philippines or the China Sea.
urbanization	The process by which towns and cities are formed and become larger as more and more people begin living and working in central areas.

Chronology

1819 CE: Sir Stamford Raffles arrives in Singapore and establishes a trading post on behalf of the British East India Company.

1826: The Straits Settlement makes Singapore, Penang, and Malacca British colonies.

1939–1945: The start of World War II brings Japan to Singapore in 1942. Singapore is badly damaged due to bombings.

1942: Singapore falls to Japan, which renames the territory Syonan, or "Light of the South."

1945: Japan is defeated in World War II and Singapore is placed back under British military rule.

1946: Singapore becomes a separate crown colony from Penang and Malacca.

1959: Lee Kuan Yew becomes prime minister of the newly self-governing Singapore.

1967: Singapore becomes a founding member of the Association of Southeast Asian Nations, better known as ASEAN.

1990: After thirty-one years in power, Prime Minister Lee Kuan Yew steps down and takes a position as senior minister. A new prime minister is elected, Goh Chok Tong.

2003: The SARS virus reaches Singapore.

2004: Lee Hsien Loong is elected prime minister.

2005: The government approves casino gambling, and S.R. Nathan begins his second term of presidency.

2006: People's Action Party wins the general elections, backing Prime Minister Lee Hsien Loong.

2011: People's Action Party wins most of Parliament, failing to secure just six seats. Tony Tan is elected to the role of president.

2014: Singapore follows the United States in regulating virtual currencies.

2015: Government regulations on banned publications are loosened, from 250 to 17.

2016: The first driverless taxi service in the world is launched in Singapore.

2017: A teenage blogger from Singapore flees to the United States and is granted asylum based on his claim of being persecuted for sharing his political opinions.

Further Reading

City Trails—Singapore. Lonely Planet Kids, 2018.

Fodor's S*ingapore 25 Best (Full-Color Travel Guide)*. Fodor's Travel, 2018.

Jong, Ria de. *Lonely Planet Singapore (Travel Guide).* Lonely Planet, 2018.

Monocle. *Singapore: The Monocle Travel Guide Series (Book 11)*. Gestalten, 2016.

Top 10 *Singapore (DK Eyewitness Travel Guide)*. DK Travel, 2018.

Internet Resources

https://www.cia.gov/library/publications/the-world-factbook/geos/sn.html
CIA World Factbook: East Asia/Southeast Asia: Singapore. Important information about Singapore.

https://www.britannica.com/place/Singapore
Singapore: Encyclopaedia Britannica. The official encyclopedia entry for Singapore.

https://www.lonelyplanet.com/singapore
Lonely Planet: Singapore. Learn about traveling to Singapore.

https://www.nationalgeographic.com/travel/destinations/asia/singapore
National Geographic Destinations: Singapore Travel Guide. Everything you need to know about traveling to Singapore.

https://www.stb.gov.sg/
Singapore Tourism Board.Singapore Tourism Board's main page.

The websites listed on this page were active at the time of publication. The publisher is not responsible for websites that have changed their addresses or discontinued operation since the date of publication. The publisher will review and update the website list upon each reprint.

Index

A
Armenian Church 55
Arts and Heritage
 Programme 79
ArtScience Museum 59, 79
Asia-Pacific Economic
 Cooperation 77
Asian Games 49

B
Bencoolen (Bengkulu) 20
British
 Crown Colony 22
 Military Administration 22
 POW 23
Bukit Batok 67, 74
 Nature Park 74, 75
Bukit Timah Nature
 Reserve 14, 15

C
Cabinet of Singapore 24
Central Catchment Nature
 Reserve 15
Chen, Georgette 58
Chen, Wen Hsi 57, 58
Chinatown 21
Chinese
 Garden 66, 71
 New Year 22
Chulia Kampong 21
Clementi 67
Clementi 69–71 69
Climate 12
Community Relations and
 Engagement
 Programme 79, 80
Constitution grants 54
 of the Republic of
 Singapore 24
Culture budget 78

D
Darussalam Mosque 70
Design Director of the
 Ministry of Design 59

E
Economic problems 41
 sectors 35
Economy 29, 77
Education 47
Efficiency Fund 41
Energy Efficiency
 Financing Programme 41
Esplanade Company
 Limited 80
Ethnic groups
 Chinese 46
 Indians 46
 Malays 46
European Town 21
Executive branch 25

F
Federation of Malaya 23
Feng Shui 54
Festivals and holidays 86
Flag of Singapore 8
Flora and fauna
 berembang 15
 common posy 16
 fairy-bluebird 16
 gecko 16
 harlequin rasbora 16
 Malayan anteater 16
 flying lemur 16
 mangrove 14, 15
 olive-winged bulbul 16
 paradise tree snake 16
 rainforest 14
 reticulated python 16
 termites 16
Flower Dome and Cloud
 Forest (glasshouses) 58
Food and drink
 bandung 51
 bubble tea 51
 chili crab 83
 chin chow 51, 53
 chin chow drink 51
 grass jelly drink 53
 Kopi-O 51, 52
 Kopi Tiam 52
 Milo Dinosaur 51, 52
 Singapore noodles 84
 street food 53
 sugarcane juice 51
 Teh Tarik 52
 tiger beer 51, 53

G
Geography of Singapore 7
Government 24
Gross Domestic Product
 (GDP) 31, 34, 77

H
High Performance Sports System, 79
Hospitality Industry 34

I
Independence 23
indigenous people (Malays) 46
Industries
  beverages 35
  biomedical products 35
  chemicals 35
  electronics 35
  equipment 35
  financial services 35
  offshore platform construction 35
  oil drilling equipment 35
  petroleum refining 35
  processed food 35
  scientific instruments 35
  ship repair 35
  telecommunication 35

J
Jiawei, Li 49
Judiciary 25
Jurong
  Bird Park 69
  East 67–69 67

K
Kallang Airport 23
Kampong Glam 22, 72–73 72
Kanagalatha (Latha) 63
Kent Ridge Park 71

L
Labor Force 34
Labrador Nature Reserve 15
Languages
  English 50
  Malay 50
  Mandarin Chinese 50
  Standard Mandarin 50
  Tamil 50
Lee Kong Chian Natural History Museum 70
Loong, Lee Hsien 26

M
Malay
  Archipelago 20
  Heritage Centre 73
Malaysia 23
Mandatory Energy Labelling 40
Members of Parliament (MPs) 25
Minimum Energy Performance Standards (MEPS) 40
Ministry of Culture, Community, and Youth 78
Mount Faber Park 71
MTV 62
Multicultural 45

N
Nanyang style 57, 58
Naomi & The Boys 61
National
  Arts Council Programme 79, 80
  Gallery Singapore 80
  Heritage Board Programme 79, 80
  Library 64
  Youth Council Programme 79, 80
Ng Teng Fong General Hospital 68
Ngon, Yeng Pway 63
North Borneo 23
Northeast Monsoon Season 13
Not Ordinarily Resident Scheme 33

O
Oasia Hotel (living tower) 60
Old Ford Motor Factory 74
Olympic Games 49
Outward Bound Singapore 80

P
Palembang 19
Party Whip 25
Pasir Ris 71–72
  Park 15, 71
People of Singapore 9
People's Action Party 23, 30
Phuc, Nguyen Xuan 26
Port of Singapore 32
President 24
Prime Minister 25
Pu Luo Chung (before Singapore) 19

93

Public Sector Taking the Lead in Environmental Sustainability (PSTLES) 38, 41
Pulau 14
  Semakau 14
  Teking 15
  Tekong 14
  Ubin 15

R
Raffles Town Plan 21
Raffles, Sir Thomas Stamford 20, 21, 73
Religions
  Buddhism 54
    Theravada 54
  Christianity 54
  Confucianism 54
  Hinduism 54
  Islam 54
    Sunni
  Taoism 54
Renewable energy
  geothermal 78
  hydroelectricity 78
  solar 78
  wind 78
Residential tax rates 32
Rock 'n' roll music 62

S
Sarawak 23
Save Energy Save Money initiative 39
School of the Arts 80
Schooling, Joseph 49
Seah, Colin 59
Selat Jurong 67

Sing, Chan Chun 25
Singapore
  Art Museum 56, 80
  Art Society 57
  Science Centre 69
  culture 45
Singapura 20
SolarNova Initiative 78
Southern Ridges 71
Southwest Monsoon Season 13
Speaker of Parliament 26
Sports
  basketball 48
  cricket 48
  sailing 48
  soccer 48
  swimming 48
  Tiger Cup 49
  waterskiing 48
Sri Mariamman Temple 54, 55
Srivijaya 19
St. John's Island 10
Sultan Mosque 72, 73
Sumatra 20
  squalls 12
Summer Olympics 49
Sungei Buhol Nature Park 15
  Wetland Reserve 15
Sungei Seletar 15

T
Tax 32
Telok Blangah Hill Park 71
Tengah 67
Tertiary Tuition Fee Scheme for Malay 80

The Quests 61
Thian Hock Keng temple 55
Tianwei, Feng 49
Timah Hill 11
Tooth Relic Temple and Museum 18
Transportation
  buses 36
  Comfort Transportation 38
  Light Rapid Transit (LRT) 37
  Mass Rapid Transit (MRT) 36, 37
  Premier Taxi 38
  Prime Taxi 38
  SBS Transit 36
  SMART Automobile 36, 38
  SMRT Taxis 38
  taxis 36
  Trans-Cab Services 38

W
Wang, Yuegu 49
Westminster System 25
World War II 22

Y
Youth Corps Singapore 80

Organizations to Contact

For general inquiries into traveling in Singapore and for brochure requests, contact:

Education USA

Stamford American International School

1 Woodleigh Lane

(Off Upper Serangoon Road)

357684 Singapore

Phone: (65) 6709 4838

https://educationusa.state.gov

STA Travel

722 Broadway, New York NY 10003.

Phone: (212) 473-6100,

Toll Free: 800-781-4040

Website: www.statravel.com

U.S. Embassy Singapore

27 Napier Road

Singapore 258508

Phone: (65) 6476-9100

Website: https://sg.usembassy.gov

Author's Biography

Catrina Daniels-Cowart is an author and illustrator living in Kentucky with her husband, two dogs, and friendly cat. She has a wide variety of interests including travel, the arts, and language. She became interested in travel after visiting Canada and moved overseas to England for several years. Today, she teaches English and encourages cultural exploration among her students.

Picture Credits

All images in this book are in the public domain or have been supplied under license by © Shutterstock.com. The publisher credits the following images as follows: Page 1 Tiep Nguyen, page 2 Tang Ian Song, page 8 Ronnie Chung, page 9 1000 words, pages 10, 45 Jordan Tan, page 13 Christian Heinz, page 15 N8 Allen, page 17 Arunee Rodloy, page 18 Natee Chalemtiragool, page 20 Makkh, page 21 Luriya Chinwan, pages 25, 68 Jay Nong, page 26 Minhtlne, page 27 Boule, page 28 Glen Photo, page 30 Robert Aug, page 31 Joachim atteldt, page 32 Delpixel, page 35 Leungchopan, page 36 2p2play, page 37 Pavol Kmeto, page 38 MK Studio, page 39 apiguide, page 40 MPanchenko, pages 41, 76 Joyfull, pages 42, 44, 50 Mentatdgt, page 43 Miki Studio, pages 46, 48 impmphoto, page 49 Leonard Zhukovsky, page 51 Zety Akhzar, page 52 Michal Hlavica, page 54 Simon HS, page 55 Oliver Fuersther, page 56 Saiko3p. page 57 Marchslim/wikimedia/private collection, page 58 Neale Consland, page 59 FoodTravel Stockforlife, page 60 diyben, pages 61, 62 Silent Wings, pages 63, 60 Tang Yan Song, page 64 userwan, page 65 Mason photography, page 66 Sarawut Kongantolech, pages 70, 74 EQ Roy, page 74 Richie Chan, page 75 Tom Carpenter, page 78 Blue Sky Studio, page 79 Creativa Images, page 81 Asia Images Group.

Front cover: © Shutterstock.com and BerryJ; vichie81; Ijam Hairi; r.nagy

To the best knowledge of the publisher, all images not specifically credited are in the public domain. If any image has been inadvertently uncredited, please notify the publisher, so that credit can be given in future printings.

Video Credits

Page 14: Kids Learning Tube, http://x-qr.net/1Lub
Page 33: Hipfig Travel-Channel, http://x-qr.net/1LdE
Page 47: Edutopia: http://x-qr.net/1LGd
Page 71: Edward Vistro:, http://x-qr.net/1Kk2